THERE'S GOLD
on TOP of that MOUNTAIN

Written by
Nelson Brown

Illustrations by
Miša Jovanović

authorHOUSE®

AuthorHouse™
1663 Liberty Drive
Bloomington, IN 47403
www.authorhouse.com
Phone: 1 (800) 839-8640

Published by AuthorHouse 02/06/2020

ISBN: 978-1-7283-3900-9 (sc)
ISBN: 978-1-7283-4587-1 (hc)
ISBN: 978-1-7283-3901-6 (e)

Print information available on the last page.

This book is printed on acid-free paper.

Scripture quotations marked NIV are taken from the Holy Bible, New
International Version®. NIV®. Copyright © 1973, 1978, 1984 by International
Bible Society. Used by permission of Zondervan. All rights reserved. [Biblica]

Ordering Information:
Quantity sales. Special discounts are available on quantity purchases by corporations,
associations, and others. For details, contact the publisher at the address above.

CONTENTS

Now to him who is able to do immeasurably more than all we ask or imagine, according to his power that is at work within us, to him be glory in the church and in Christ Jesus throughout all generations, for ever and ever! Amen." Ephesians 3:20-21

DEDICATION

*T*here are many people whom I dedicate this book to. If I forgot anyone, I apologize. I hope this book impacts your lives as much as you have impacted mine. I'll start with my mother, Mary Brown. She is the woman who has been there for me my entire life. She loves people and really has a good heart! When you call her voice mail, it ends with her phrase, *"There's never a wrong time to do the right thing!"*

My son Marcel and daughter Myah. Do your best with your gifts, be kind and respectful to others, and you will both attain everything you desire.

My family of Brown's and Fair's. Here we go: Uncles: Neal, Lawrence, Carly (Berdia), Epp, Joe, Ted, Stan, Marvin, Danny. (Deceased – Fred, Greg, Donald, Darryl, Leon. Isaac, Harry, Bob, Fred Woods). Aunts: Harriet, Laverne, Karen, Lois, Amy, Brenda, Mildred, Marilyn, and Ann (Deceased – Vivian, Barbara. Lynn)

Cousins: Al, Tina, Michelle (Rodney), Felicia, Aleta, Monique, Jerome, Pookey, Vonette, Lisa, Leslie, Valerie, Aaron, Hari, Krysnavati, Brebre, Yaz, Kenesha, Dez, Alexandria, Rodney Jr., CC, Nathan, Warren, Mike, Ricky, Raymon, Rosheen, Vincent, Greg Jr., Carley Jr., Tracy, Terri, Alicia, Tonya, Dee, Wes (Denice), Diana my sister, Stacey,

Tiffany, Alan, Alex, Fred, Jason, Nicki (deceased – Maurice, Tierra) and all of your children!

Friends: Chris, Tasha, Rick Jordan, Reginald Burnette (Teresa), Big Rich, Bill Blackburn, Dr. D, Gus, Karen (Blue), Mrs. Harris, Norman Holley, Annie, Dee Hall, Tammy, Donna Nelson, Lori, Arlene, Vido, and all the rest!

Stockbridge Family: Jennifer, Valerie, Michelle, Bevy, TB, Patti, Phil, Chris Dorsey, Shelley, Gary Robinson, Scutter, The Jacksons, The Evans, (deceased – Mr. Doggett). & Mrs. Doggett, (deceased Mr. Burns) & Mrs. Burns, and all the rest!

INTRODUCTION

When my daughter was about 6 years old, I knew she would graduate high school in the year 2020. With that said, I began thinking about 2020 and her graduation before the year came. I imagined her ceremony and the class talking about the year 2020 and what it stood for.

I'm not certain, but I believe most people in the United States have gone to the eye doctor to have their eyes checked. In the optometry world, the eye chart 20/20 represents perfect vision. To add to the thought of my daughter graduating in 2020, and what it stood for, one has to be focused in order to have perfect vision. I truly want everyone to have 20/20 vision for their lives.

When I was in the third grade, Mrs. Thomas, the teacher at Lafayette Elementary School in Cleveland Ohio, shared with my parents, "Nelson is a smart young man who needs to attend Harvey Rice, an enrichment school for gifted children." My parents wanted the best for me, so they made the decision to transfer me to a different school.

I was not pleased with the decision at all! It meant being away from my cousins and friends. It meant going to a strange place I knew nothing of, and I was scared. I was eight. However, my parent's focus was for me to get a better education. After all, it was free!

During my fourth and fifth grade years, while attending Harvey Rice, I learned French. I would try to impress my friends and family by saying, *"Comment allez-vous."* It's kind of pronounced "Come on talley vu!" Try it! It means, *"How are you?"*

You just learned French! It may be small, but it could be just what you needed to begin to learn a new language.

Living a full life is similar to learning a second language. It's tough enough learning one language, but to take on a second one can feel like an impossible task. There are many people who would probably say, *"It's too hard"* before they ever tried. Go back and read that *French* sentence again. It wasn't hard at all! You probably never tried before. Once you did, you realized it was easy!

It's not that living a full life is hard. Not truly living makes it hard. Life is supposed to be challenging. It challenges us in order to grow emotionally, mentally, and to have a better quality of life. Living a full life gives us the opportunity to become the best version of ourselves if we believe it.

If you've ever witnessed a baby chicken hatching, you would realize the entire process is a struggle for the little chick. He has to push, peck, and stretch out to break the shell. By doing so, his wings and legs get stronger. When he's out, he's walking and ready for life!

What if a person saw the little chick having a hard time, and decided to help him out by breaking away pieces of the shell? Do you realize the chick would probably never walk and eventually die! Why? It needed the struggle to live.

Living a full life has its ups and downs. Those ups and down periods can feel unfair to many. If you've ever felt circumstances were unfair, you're probably right. However, we still must continue to do our best. I believe *those who are challenged the most and overcome the struggles, will live the best.*

Challenges and obstacles are needed. They affect and benefit our overall health and wellness. They reveal themselves as conflicts we may have, goals we want to accomplish, a need or situation to address, or an unfulfilled idea or dream. When these roadblocks come up, in order to grow and thrive, we make daily choices to move beyond them.

Some people make the decision to face their challenges in some areas, but not all. However, there are many who have fears, doubts, and worries about how, or even if they will face the obstacle or challenge. Often, the thought of the "possible outcome" prevents people from even trying. Don't worry. You're not alone.

Those challenges, fears, doubts, worries, and struggles, could look like a number of things. For example, a person who wants to learn a new skill or continue in school may feel like it's not possible (doubt). Someone could be in a bad relationship and see no way of getting out, or fixing it (fear). Maybe you're unemployed, disabled, poor, single, emotionally hurt, wanting to change careers, making a choice about the military, incarcerated, or whatever your circumstances are. There are emotions and feelings which can stop you dead in your tracks and prevent you from ever changing your situation for the better, if you allow it.

"There's Gold on Top of that Mountain" is first about understanding your life is a wonderful journey to experience and thrive in. It's about pursuing those *positive* ideas you have without allowing anything to stop you. It's recognizing what's before you and choosing to go beyond it. It's how we face those challenges, struggles, fears, and obstacles, which give us the strength to conquer them, and become the best person we can be.

This book begins by showing you symbolic obstacles we all face. My hope is, with truth, honesty about who you are, where you are, and a strong belief in where you want to go, you will build the courage and strength to face and conquer your own barriers. I want you to experience more victories in 2020 so you can live the life you've always wanted.

G.O.L.D = Getting Our Life's Desires

WHO IS THIS BOOK FOR?

*T*his book is for anyone, regardless of age, gender, race, or nationality, who has any ideas, personal achievements, or passions that are unresolved, or unfulfilled. It's for those who still have goals about anything. It's for those who feel there is something missing in their life. It's for those who know within themselves they didn't give it their all in some area of their life, but still have the constant reminder. If so, and that's you, this book is for you. I've listed some questions here for some who may wonder if this book is for them. If any apply to you or anyone you know, this book may help.

Is there anyone in your life you'd like to have a better relationship with, but no progress has taken place?

Is your job not fulfilling, but you haven't taken steps to change it?

Have you thought about continuing your education but have doubts or concerns?

Do you want to improve your health, but you keep backsliding or can't seem to stay on track?

Do you have an idea for a business, but you haven't taken a step to do anything beyond the idea?

Do you own or manage a business and want your team's performance to improve?

Do you want your children to do better in school?

Do you want your relationship with your significant other to improve and you're not sure how to express it?

Have you had thoughts of sadness, or anger because you feel your life is not what you wanted it to be and you don't know what to do?

Do you feel there's more to you, but you're not doing anything to discover it?

You're making good money, but other areas in your life are suffering. How can you improve them as well?

You're in a bad relationship and feel stuck. How can you move on?

You're in the military or incarcerated, and not confident about what you'll do once you separate or released.

Does your past haunt you and keep you down?

Do you struggle defining your true purpose?

Is there an addiction you're challenged with and you're looking for a resource to help battle through and overcome it?

Personally, *"There's Gold on Top of That Mountain"* is for everyone. It doesn't matter if you're the CEO of a large corporation who wants to improve your health, or the 16-year-old boy who likes the girl in the seat next to him, but is afraid to say anything. This book can help you move forward.

With this said, I'm believing this book should be in the hands of everyone who has anything they want to improve or accomplish. I know you will get what you desire.

AUTHOR'S MESSAGE

I wrote this book because I had too. In the last few years, it has been an idea that stayed with me no matter what was going on, or what I was personally going through. I just couldn't shake it or ignore it. It has been like this continuous knock on my heart saying, "Nelson, write this book!"

I believe people are connected. We're all uniquely made, but we're also very similar. If you've ever seen an orange grove with thousands of trees lined up, although they are all separate, we know they are all connected. No one tree will look exactly the same, but they all have leaves, branches, and oranges. They have different shapes and sizes but each one produces fruit. Some fruit is sweeter than others, but still, producing fruit. We're not much different.

Our entire physical makeup is very similar. Our outer skin, bone structure, nerves, and inner parts were created very similarly. People who are considered "normal" all have the same physical components as everyone else. The difference is color, size, and shapes, but basically, we are the same.

The population of people who have disabilities and illnesses are unique. However, they are also the same in how they were created. I believe some individuals who have more physical challenges to overcome, are equipped with more internal strength to thrive if they choose to. Anyone who appears to lack in one area may also have more strength in other areas, if they decide to unlock it.

Our emotions, feelings, thoughts, and other mental components are also very similar. All of us experience different levels of fear, doubt, worry, courage, strength, and all the other feelings people have. We just experience these feelings in different ways.

Just like the orange grove is connected and produces fruit, we are all connected and have the ability to produce fruit. The fruit we produce is in the form and quality of the life we live, and what we create with it. It can be bad or good based on the choices we make throughout our life.

Every human on the planet has the ability to do or become something greater in their life if they choose to! Every one of us has dreams, ideas, and passions in life. Every one of us can love, and care for others. Every one of us, given the opportunity, can accomplish more in our life. This is our true connection.

There's Gold on Top of That Mountain is not a story I simply made up one day. It came to me. It was given to me. It had to be shared. It's part of my contribution to my friends, family, and the rest of the world.

Someone may ask, *"Who do you think you are to be able to share this kind of information?"* My response is, *"I'm just the person this project was given to. I could have ignored and agreed that I'm not capable and simply disregarded the idea, but I couldn't. It wouldn't let me set it aside. I had to do this!"*

I have personally experienced every obstacle in this story in one way or another. Just like I know humans are all connected and have more in common than not, I believe every one of us experiences similar struggles and obstacles in life. The challenges are different, but everybody on the planet has to face, and overcome something in life to be able to move beyond it, and accomplish their goals.

It has taken me over 40 years to realize what held me back from achieving my dreams. I could fault others if I chose to, but the reality was, it had more to do with my lack of honesty, belief, trust, and faith in myself, and the choices I made along the way.

It's easy to live life hiding the whole truth of yourself. We can take little pieces of ourselves and hide them away for a lifetime. As a matter of fact, I fooled myself into believing my life was just fine by burying the hurt and pain that was deep inside of me. Doing so prevented me from living up to my full potential and having a better quality of life. The result was, I didn't experience my best. I existed and lived. Does that sound familiar? Once I came to grips with my truth, I was able to stand and continue to pursue what I believed I was created for.

For you, know that you still have time to accomplish what you truly desire. I often share with people I interact with, *"As long as you have breath in your body, you can achieve what's in your heart."*

As you read this book, along the way, think of areas that either have held you back from your greatest version of yourself, and write them here as you read. If you are bold enough to be honest with yourself, and accept the challenge, I believe you can begin your quest discovering *"The gold on top of your mountain!"*

In the creation of this project, I have included several scriptures from the bible that resonate for me. This is not a religious book. The truth is, many motivational and inspirational speakers received *much* of their wisdom from the bible. Some just don't acknowledge the origin of their information. I am.

Some people who don't acknowledge their spirituality, may assume the bible is a bunch of religious nonsense which keeps them from enjoying their life. I disagree. I believe it contains wisdom and truth about how to make the best of the life we have, no matter what your personal beliefs are. The verses I have chosen can be very powerful in helping you achieve your gold.

"There's Gold on Top of That Mountain" is a story of triumph. However, it doesn't start that way. It starts with a man entering a new town and sharing some news for an adventure which will prosper those who are willing to join. As you will read, many of the people begin to justify why they cannot continue the journey.

Let's see if you have anything in common with the people from the story in the beginning. If you do, it's okay. *Knowing and being honest with yourself is the first step to the best of the rest of your life.* Enjoy!

THE JOURNEY

*H*e came into town with sparkling dust on his feet. All the town's people wondered why this old man had this shiny glow all over his feet. He stood in the middle of the town and shouted, "There's gold on top of that mountain!"

The people looked at him with disapproval in their eyes. He turned to them again and shouted, "There's gold on top of that mountain!" As he shouted, he pointed to a mountain in the distance.

Someone in the crowd shouted back, "There's no gold on top of that mountain. You're just saying so!"

The old man turned to the young man and said, "Young man, have you ever been to that mountain?" The young man replied in a soft low voice, "No, but that doesn't matter." The old man replied, "I'm standing before you with sparkling dust covering my feet. My sack is filled with gold. I'm right here shouting and sharing information that could make you rich beyond your wildest dreams, and you stand there doubting me when you have never been outside of these gates!"

The young man shouted back, "Why should we believe you? You could have covered yourself with paint just to trick us! Then, when we left to go for the gold, you would take everything from us."

Obstacle #1 – Imagining the worst result to justify not trying.

Another young boy who stood nearby said, "Why would that old man take all that time to paint himself in gold just to trick us so he could rob us? What would he rob? We're a poor town?" The old man turned to the young boy and smiled. He then shouted again, "*There's gold on top of that mountain*! I'm going back for more. Who will be bold enough to join me?"

One by one each person in the crowd thought of a reason not to go. "It's too cold to climb a mountain," shouted one person. "It's too cold!"

"It's too high!"

"We don't have time!"

"We don't have the tools!"

One by one they all made excuses then walked away until there were only ten people - five boys and five girls.

The old man turned and said, "All of you who have decided to take this journey with me will be rich beyond your wildest dreams if you finish the trip. Let's go!"

They all started to leave, and just as they were outside of the gate, one of the boys turned and said, *"I changed my mind. I thought about it, and I don't want to take a chance, so count me out*! **It looks too far"** – Obstacle two.

The old man said, *"When you first start on your journey, only look at the first step, and not the whole journey. Doing so will help you make the second step."* Then, there were nine.

As the remaining nine people made it down the hill, they saw they had to travel through the woods. None of them had ever come this far. When they were closer to the woods, one of the girls turned and said, *"I won't be able to see where I'm going. I changed my mind and don't want to take a chance so count me out.* I can't see making it through.

Getting past the trees. Obstacle three.

The old man turned to the group and said, *"Sometimes it's hard to see what's ahead, but if you keep going, you will make it through."* Then, there were eight.

2 Corinthians 5:7 – For we walk by faith, not by sight

When they came out of the woods, everyone was relieved. They all kept going.

They came to a bridge that was high above the ground. One of the boys turned to the group and said, "*This is too high, and I don't trust this bridge. I changed my mind and don't want to take a chance so count me out!*" **Crossing a bridge**. Obstacle four.

The old man turned to the group and said, "There will often come a time when you have to leave one place to get to the other side. It may seem safer to stay on one side but if you never cross, you'll never know what could be waiting for you that's better."

Then, there were seven.

When the remaining people crossed over the bridge, they were all relieved and kept going.

As they continued on, the remaining group saw a river they had to pass. One of the girls turned to the group and said, *"I can't swim. I changed my mind and don't want to take a chance so count me out. The current looks too strong!"*

The old man turned to the group and said, *"Currents may look powerful in your life. As you walk through them, you will plant yourself and become more assured as you pass through. You just have to keep moving."*

They all started to walk in the river and realized they were able to withstand the current. When they crossed over, they were all relieved and kept going. **Facing the currents.** Obstacle five.

Then, there were six.

As nightfall approached, one of the girls turned to the group and said, *"It's getting dark and I'm afraid. I changed my mind and don't want to take a chance so count me out! When it gets dark, I'm scared!"*

The old man turned to the group and said, *"Darkness may fall on us all. But don't be afraid because the light always follows darkness."* **Darkness**. Obstacle six.

Then, there were five.

Romans 13:12 – The light is far gone; the day is at hand. So then let us cast off the works of darkness and put on the armor of light.

The next morning, everyone woke up and it was daytime. They were all relieved and kept going.

When they kept walking, they noticed clouds were beginning to form and a bolt of lightning crossed the sky.

One of the boys turned to the group and said, *"I don't like when the clouds form. We might get struck by lightning and get hurt or die! I changed my mind and don't want to take a chance so count me out!"*

The old man turned to the remaining group and said, *"In life, there will be times when a storm is on the way and clouds form. But, if you believe you can make it through and keep going, you'll realize that a few clouds can't stop your progress."*

A storm is forming. Obstacle seven.

Then, there were four.

2 Corinthians 4: 8-9 We are afflicted in every way, but not crushed; perplexed, but not driven to despair; persecuted, but not forsaken; struck down, but not destroyed.

The remaining group kept going and sure enough, the clouds eventually cleared, and the lightning stopped.

As they continued on their journey, the ground beneath them showed some cracks. In front of them, the entire ground had a long crack that separated the earth. In order to go on, they had to jump over. One person turned to the group and said, *"I can't see myself jumping over this. I'm afraid I won't make it. I changed my mind and don't want to take a chance so count me out!"*

The old man turned to the remaining group and said, *"There will often come a time when you will have to believe in something you can do before you see the result. That leap of faith will help you trust and succeed."* **Taking the leap**. Obstacle eight.

Then, there were three.

Hebrews 11:1 – Now faith is confidence in what we hope for and assurance about what we do not see.

The last group made the leap and continued on their journey. They called out for the other person to make the jump, but she didn't turn around.

Before the group knew it, they were at the bottom of the mountain. Just then, one of the boys turned to the remaining group and said, *"I'm tired. It just looks too high to climb up and I don't want to fall now. I changed my mind and don't want to take a chance so count me out!"*

The old man turned to the group and said, *"When you're standing right in front of your goal is the time where you may want to give up. It can appear to be too big. Just hang in there!"* **Standing in front of the goal.** Obstacle nine.

Then, there were two.

Galatians 6:9 – And let us not grow weary of doing good, for in due season we will reap, if we do not give up

The last two people started to climb the mountain. As they were closer to the top, the last girl slipped and was about to fall.

Just then, the old man reached out to her and said, *"This is where many people who are about to achieve their goal often need a little help. Take my hand. No one can really make it in this world on their own. You came this far, and the truth is, I have always been here. I wanted to see how persistent you would be. I will help you now."*

In that moment, the little girl took the old man's hand and he pulled her to the top. The girl and the old man both helped the boy up as well.

As they stood on top of the mountain, the boy and girl looked around and saw all the chests of gold. They had overcome every obstacle that was before them. Each of the others had the exact same challenges, however, for various reasons, they could not overcome them.

The last two broke the chains and now would be rich beyond their wildest dreams. More than rich, they had earned wealth in the course of their journey. They realized their gold on top of the mountain.

The old man turned to them both and said, *"You see. If you never give up on what you want, no matter what comes your way, you will achieve your goals and can live a good life."*

They smiled and were amazed at all their gold.

The end…

No, it's not the end. Many times in life, a person has their own gold they hope to achieve one day. As children, we think anything is possible. But what happens as we get older? Our dreams become fogged with the troubles of life. We begin to justify why the earlier picture changed. Honestly, your reasoning may seem like it's justified. What happened or didn't happened is true. However, it no longer has to keep you from your true desires and goals.

The fear of *what could be* can be very strong only when we allow it to stay in our heart. Concerns of *what might happen* often cause many people to simply give up, ignore, or forget about their dream.

I want to talk about each of the obstacles in this story. By doing so, perhaps you can take a deeper look at yourself and fight through any beliefs which could be limiting your own journey in life.

REFLECTION

*T*he first obstacle began in the town where many of the people were living with fear. To justify the fear, one of the town's people who spoke for others, created the worst scenario he could think of. In his mind, he imagined the bad in the old man without knowing anything about him. By creating this false truth, it gave him the ammunition he needed to not take the journey.

People will make up stories and make claims which are totally false to stay within their circle of fear and keep them from moving forward in life. They want others to believe as they do. If others don't investigate for themselves, they will believe the false claims and believe the same.

By using a false truth to justify a position, and defending it, we can create an invisible bubble around us. It doesn't allow anything in, and we keep ourselves sheltered from experiencing any different life outside of it. Here are some examples: Our family, friends, people who look like us, (meaning race) jobs, created values, beliefs, and attitudes.

Here is an example of how a false truth can impact people. Let's say you are a green person. As a green person, you have your close relationships with other green people. At work, you are more comfortable with green people. Wherever you go, you look for the green people because you believe you relate better with them simply because they are green. You have no desire to know others, although you've seen many blue, pink, orange, and purple people. Since you are green, you believe green is better than any other color and you avoid them without personally knowing anything about the other colors.

The false truth may reveal itself as you justify why you don't associate with the blue, pink, and purple people. One may say, "I heard the blue people steal, or purple people have bad manners. Using these *"false truths"* justifies your resentment of the other wonderful colors of people. It confirms you wanting to stay within your own group.

You are living in a *"green"* people bubble and you believe you are safer and happier there. With this belief, your entire life, you rarely have any real experiences or connections with anyone other than green people. If you do, those relationships are usually very superficial like saying "good morning" without a smile or eye contact.

You can choose that life, but it limits experiencing people. It limits reaching outside of your green bubble to realize other people have thriving lives as well. It's not just about green. Interestingly though, you may know in your heart you have many green people you don't care for. But, because they are green like you, you tolerate and pretend to be okay with them.

In your heart, you may feel you'd love to connect with other people but limit experiencing them because of what the other green people may think of you. Truthfully, many green people are wanting the same.

Many of the town's people had the "green people bubble belief." They lived their entire life inside the gates because they were simply afraid to experience anything outside of it. So, when the old man said, *"There's gold on top of that mountain,"* all of the people, except for the ten, justified staying within the town, never to experience any life outside of those gates.

Is that you? Are you living in a "green" people bubble? You don't have to stay there. You can begin to have a new belief, reach out, and experience other wonderful people. Get out and see exciting new places. Go for it and you will see the fear you used to justify your beliefs was just one big lie to hold you back!

In the next section, I'm going to focus on each of the remaining obstacles. It's time for you to overcome all of your own obstacles in 2020 and beyond so you can experience *"The gold on top of your mountain!"*

Feel free to list some beliefs you truly believe could be limiting your growth.

1)_____

2)_____

3)_____

4)_____

5)_____

OBSTACLE #2 - IT LOOKS TOO FAR

When the children who decided to go on the journey for the gold, one child was barely out of the village when he looked again and decided the distance was too far to try. Many people who have a goal will never attempt to pursue it because to reach it seems impossible or too far. Has this ever happened to you?

If you are bold enough, take a second here, and right down a few areas in your life where you thought about something you wanted to do, but never tried. This is your time to look deep within you and begin to make those hidden ideas and dreams resurface. You know they are there! Write down at least three:

1)_____

2)_____

3)_____

If you couldn't think of three goals, that's ok. One is a good place to start.

What do you believe the reason in your life is that prevented you from starting? There are many reasons people don't start what they said they would. Only you know your truth. I made a few discoveries by investigation, having conversations with people who were bold enough to share, and by taking a hard look at myself.

What I've discovered is sometimes the *"thing"* we want to accomplish sounds good to say, but there has to be constant effort applied towards it. When we look at the effort we have to put in, just the image or thought of the effort stops us before we start. It looks too far. For instance, one might say they want to lose 20 pounds in 6 months. Well, it sounds good to say. We say it then feel good we voiced it. We'll think about what it will take. Then it stops cold. Nothing! Sound familiar?

It's easy to talk yourself out of trying. For some, it might simply seem to be too hard! Isn't it amazing how we can talk ourselves out of pursuing something because of how we think it will turn out? What really happens when we don't even try? And, as a result of not trying, what are we really left with?

When we don't make an attempt, one can fool themselves into believing the circumstance would stay the same. It doesn't! It may appear to stay the same but, in reality, it gets worse! What do you think happened to the boy in the story who didn't try? He probably went back to the town and made up a story as to why he didn't try. Does that sound familiar to you?

Don't let this be your story. I want you to begin to pursue those ideas and goals you wrote down. I also like to, as they say, "keep it real" so you can make progress and become the best version of yourself.

After you've written down those few areas, start by simply picking one to work with. Yep, just one. Having too many goals or ideas can stop you right away. Let's keep it simple and pick one to start. Second, try not to look at the big picture in the beginning. That's what stopped the little boy in the story. He looked out the gate and imagined the whole journey as being too much, so why even try? When we look at the end goal, it can seem overwhelming. Instead, break it down into little sections. Take small steps for the progress and only think about the small steps at a time.

Say you had this idea about cooking a new recipe. The recipe has many ingredients and steps to take before it can become that delicious meal on a plate. Get each ingredient first. You won't complete it without the ingredients but, you must start by gathering what you need.

Knowing you start somewhere, and being okay with wherever you begin your journey, is the first step that sets up taking the second step. Everyone starts from a beginning.

List a first simple first step you can make right here. Take it!

1)_____

What could be a second step?

2)_____

Once you take the second step, you are ready to take the third, fourth, and so on. You just have to keep going. You'll get there.

OBSTACLE #3 – GETTING PAST THE TREES

*T*here is a saying which goes, "A person can't see the forest for the trees." The saying suggests a person can't see the big picture of an idea because they are too focused on the small details. In this story, one of the children could not continue into the forest. Her rationale was the belief she wouldn't be able to see where she were going, so instead of trying, she quit.

There are people who will begin a goal, but because they can't see the end, or come across a blockage, instead of continuing, they give up. They may say, *"I was doing fine until it was blocked."* In life there are going to be events that may seem to block you from achieving your dream. With some of those events, you won't have a clear picture of how to get past them. Just keep going.

I've seen firsthand how a person can be focused on a dream they want, and then all types of things start happening. For example, you want to go back to school in the fall because your education has been important to you but for some reason, every time you get ready to start, something happens. Maybe someone close to you became ill, or your car broke down, or you had a breakup in your relationship. Events like these can cause one to stop in their tracks.

Understand, there will always be something or someone who will appear to block you from pursuing your goals. Events happen. You should decide that no matter what happens or attempts to block you, you will keep going.

You want to accomplish whatever goal you have for yourself. I've heard people say, "I'm doing it for my kids, or other family members, or some other cause." While this may be true, ultimately, I believe, doing it for yourself will be more rewarding and powerful. As I mentioned earlier, you can't allow anything to stop you. Trust me. There will be reasons which appear true and could present themselves as reasonable to stop. However, you must trust and believe the goal you want will improve the quality of your life. It doesn't always have to be financial either. If it makes you feel better, *see it through and make it through. The choice is up to you!*

List a few goals you began, but feel something blocked you from completing. Push through and bring them back to life.

1)_____

2)_____

3)_____

OBSTACLE #4 – CROSSING THE BRIDGE

*T*he third child would not cross the bridge. There will be times in the process of pursuing what you desire for your

life, you'll get to a point where you must leave one side and take the chance to go to the other side. When you go to the other side, you are choosing to leave something behind. When you are pursuing your goals, crossing the bridge is more about trust. The bridge sits high off the ground and it can appear to consume you with fear which could stop your progress.

Have you ever walked or driven across a bridge? It can be a terrifying experience or an exciting one. It just depends on how you look at it. I know people who will avoid crossing a bridge even though it's the same width as a regular road and extremely sturdy. Even a bridge that sits between a ridge that has been around for many years is sturdy enough for a person to cross. However, being assured of its sturdiness and reliability, many still won't cross.

Crossing a bridge in this story was the only way to continue on the destination. It's an obstacle that has to be overcome. Some people can view a bridge as crossing over from life to death. The fear of something going wrong is a battle and constant worry. Because of the fear, some never cross. Does that sound familiar to you? Is there a bridge in your life you are afraid to cross because you think it will mean losing something you've held on to?

When you take that walk and have faith in what you're pursuing, it's not going from life to death, it's leaving death for life!

If you're engaged in an activity you believe isn't producing true value and honor for your life, or something which is preventing you from making a positive change in your life, you're really held captive from your potential. It's a trap! It may appear to be the place where you want to be, but in actuality, it's keeping you from having the real life that's better for you, and others you love.

While you're stuck on one side, you really know inside that it's not where you want to be. Being in a place where you know you really don't want to be can feel like a bad wound. You feel this pain in you. It's getting worse, and it hurts. However, you do nothing about it until it eventually discourages you and any progress.

You may not be physically wounded but, mentally, emotionally, and spiritually, you are hurt until one day the wound does permanent damage and leaves you on the side of life you don't want to be on. Crossing over is saying, *"I don't want to be hurt and discouraged any longer. I want to live!"* Crossing over is truly going from death to life!

Take a moment and write down what area in your life you want to leave and cross over.

1)_____

2)_____

3)_____

OBSTACLE #5 - FACING THE CURRENT

Currents have the ability to shape our lives. Rushing water is always changing and is never the same at any given point. Your life will have many currents and they

will not look like any others. Currents are the challenges we must face in order to get past and get on with life.

The young lady in the story, although she had the courage to overcome the previous challenges, when she was faced with something that seemed to be moving too fast and constantly changing, she could not continue.

This rushing water current can be one of the most confusing obstacles because it is the only one that is moving and changing constantly - Just like life. Just like the rushing current, it doesn't wait for anyone or anything, and it never slows down.

In life, we don't always get to choose the currents we face. However, we do get the freedom to decide how to get through the current. As the saying goes, *"We don't get to choose what happens to us, but we do get to choose how we respond to what happens to us."* We just get through it.

When you are faced with a rushing current along your journey, you can decide to not go through it if you want to, but the journey will be delayed and you'll have to find another way. If you never go through your currents, the problems will never go away. Your personal growth will be hindered.

The rushing current may knock you down. It may take you under for a little while, but get up, plant yourself with a sturdy foot, and take another strong step. You will realize eventually you made it through and built strength along the way.

Imaging the successful feeling of making it. The thought alone will keep you going until you make it through.

When life appears to be rushing at you and it seems like too much to handle, take a moment to realize if you just dig in, and take those steps to get through it, you will pass it, and be able to continue. You might get a little wet. It may even exhaust you some. However, it will be worth it in the end. Just take a strong step to get through it!

Remember, water heals as well. The current you fight through just might be what you need to heal from any affliction you may have faced.

What current do you need to fight through?

1)_____

2)_____

3)_____

OBSTACLE #6 - DARKNESS

Of all the obstacles and challenges that can stop us in our tracks, I most definitely believe the one which can change your entire life if you allow it, the one that can cause the most damage, and the one that can have an impact you long after you've left this earth is darkness. In the story, when the child didn't want to continue because it had become dark, the old man turned to her and said, *"Darkness may fall on us all."* This is a true statement.

Darkness can prevent one from attaining their goal because it can appear to drain you, and all of your energy. It's like it zaps you into doing nothing. It can give you that "I don't care or I don't feel like it" mentality. Darkness can take you into a place where you believe no one cares, no one wants you, and everyone is against you. If you've ever been there, you know I'm speaking the truth. Sometimes we are there and don't realize it.

Darkness can look like hate for someone or a group of people. Darkness can be a hidden anger or a deep fear. It can appear as a sadness that you may not feel all the time, but enough to where you just can't seem to accomplish anything. The point is; darkness can and will keep you from ever experiencing your best self if you allow it.

The truth is, darkness is part of life just like everything else. When I talk to people, I share with them, *"It's not that darkness itself takes you out. What takes you out is the length of time you stay there."* In my opinion, the difference between some chronic health conditions is the length of time a person stays there. We will all have dark periods in our life.

A dark period can be putting man's best friend down. His name was Trouble. He was the biggest, goofiest, best dog I'd ever had. He was so animated and funny. He was a Bullmastiff mixed with who knows what. Trouble was always into trouble! His name was perfect for him. Trouble could also be extremely vicious to anyone or anything who walked past our home. People literally crossed the street to avoid our home if Trouble was outside. His bark and growl were terrifying. But he was like a big ole softie with all of us in the house. In his 9 years with us, he never, not once, ever showed any aggression towards the family.

When Trouble became ill, his energy level went from 100 miles an hour to zero. We took him to the veterinarian, and they told us in short, there was nothing they could do.

Putting him down was one of the saddest days of my life. I think I cried for two weeks. More than a few times, my daughter and I cried together. When I spoke of Trouble to others, a sadness came upon me where I almost cried again. Those sad moments are healthy. Anytime we lose a loved one, the sadness or grief that comes with it is normal.

During that time, I wasn't productive at all. My motivation and energy were gone. I know it was just a dog, but I loved that dog. The experience caused me to temporarily shut down in every area. It happens to us all.

What's key to remember is we will all have dark experiences. It's important to know those times don't have to last long. As long as we keep the hope, it will be there when we think it won't.

I've talked about darkness long enough. The good news is light always follows darkness if you allow it. What does that mean? Doesn't the sun always rise? Darkness will go away when you make up your mind to move beyond it. And when it does go away, or when you decide the dark period in your life needs to end, know the good times and best times will show up.

So how do we get past this obstacle? I'm going to make it really simple because it actually is. You realize what's happening in the moment and allow it to only impact you for that moment. Then ask yourself, "What can I do to get out of this slump?"

One way to get out of a slump is to do something for someone else. That's right! To take the darkness out of your life, you can be the light for someone else. Find someone you can do something for. When you help someone else, you will discover a load has been lifted or a peak of light has showed up in your life. *The more you do to brighten someone else's day, the brighter yours will become.* I guarantee! Then, you keep moving forward. It really is that simple. You just need to see it that way.

If you are experiencing a dark period in your life, list a few areas where you can be a light in another person's life right now.

1)_____

2)_____

3)_____

OBSTACLE #7 – THE STORM IS FORMING

The storm that forms in our lives can cause us to freeze up and be overcome with doubt because of the unknown. In the story, the one kid saw the clouds forming and the lightning then decided he had seen enough. This obstacle can be very misleading in a person's life.

How many times have you turned on the television or lived in an area where the news caster comes on and says, *"There is a storm forming in the Atlantic and it looks like it's going to be pretty rough!"* Then, the reporter shows a video of people gathering sandbags, extra water, and other items to prepare for the storm. Sometimes the storm is severe, but often there is minimum damage done. The news rarely reports when there wasn't much damage. That's not news. It's only appears to be news when there is mass destruction of property or life.

In our lives, there can be many storms that seem to be on the way. Our thoughts about what could "possibly" go wrong can stop us in our tracks. We can talk ourselves right out of accomplishing anything by thinking about what could go wrong. We create our own storm on a bright and sunny day.

Have you ever tried to accomplish a task for yourself you'd put off, then decided to tackle it, only to discover everything is going wrong on that day? *The storm forming.* Your car didn't start up. *The storm forming.* A friend called you with an emergency. *The storm forming.* Your job wants you to work overtime when you had plans. *The storm forming.* The cat died. *Storm forming.* Family has to come live with you because of poor choices they made. *The storm forming.* All these storms forming on the day you decided to take action. Ever heard the expression, "If it can go wrong, it will go wrong!" *Storms forming.*

What do you do when the storm is forming? You recognize it. In areas like Florida, Texas, and others states that are known for storms, when the news is on and they are being informed, they turn to each other and say, "The storm is coming! We have to prepare!" People take action! They go purchase batteries and food to be ready just in case the storm does catastrophic damage.

You also have the group of people who say, *"No big deal! I'm gonna ride it out because other storms have hit and nothing happened."* This group of people see trouble coming and do nothing. They never do. They believe no good can come from their life because storms always come around so no need to ever do anything.

Then you have the storm chasers. Those who say, *"I've never seen a Tornado up close, let's go where it is so we can get a closer look."* This group of people are too busy looking for storms in other people's lives. They instigate, gossip, and are so busy looking for trouble, they never do anything about their own lives. In every case, people made a decision.

We don't always have the same amount of time to prepare for the storms that impact us. They may happen quickly. That's ok. You just respond a little faster. You know it's on the way and you say, *"I see this storm but it is not going to stop me!"*

Here is a fact. I only have control 100 percent of the choices I make, and 0 control over the choice others make. When a storm is brewing, it may not be something that's in your control. It may be a barrier out of your control. You just have patience, remain calm, and stay persistent. No need to panic. Realize if there is something out of your complete control, you have to respond differently until you can be in control again. Once you do, you can then proceed on your journey.

A storm can also be thought of or looked at as a necessity of life. When a storm comes, although it may cause damage, it can also be seen as a cleansing. It washes away the old and gives the planet a chance to start fresh.

In life, a storm can be a chance to get rid of old crippling thoughts, people, or behaviors. It can wash away and create a new opportunity, relationship, career, or any other trouble you've had to endure. A storm can cleanse and create an entirely new path.

Are there any storms in your path? If so, what are they, and what can you do to prepare?

1)_____

2)_____

3)_____

OBSTACLE #8 – TAKING THE LEAP OF FAITH

*I*n the story, there was a young person who came upon the large crack in the ground. The only way to get past it was to take a leap and jump over it. Unlike any of the other obstacles, there was nothing beneath the person to keep them from falling if they didn't succeed in taking the leap. But the only way to know if you can accomplish something when there is a chance you could fail or fall, is to have courage, faith and belief. There is so much power in simply believing you can.

I share with people all the time, *"If you believe what you say to yourself then it's true!* If you believe you can't do something, you are right! If you believe you're stressed, worried, won't get the job, or whatever it is, you are correct! But if you believe you can do it, you're capable, you will get the job, you are also correct!

When you *"go for it"* and succeed, there is an emotion that will come over you that makes you feel good. It's that *"I did it"* feeling you will have no matter how small the leap was. When you are successful in one *"leap of faith"* it will empower you to take another, and another, and keep on going.

Too many times people focus on the *"What if I don't make it"* mentality. *Thinking you won't will most likely cause you to fail.* You, or someone else will say, *"I told you so!"* Ever heard those words? Often, the "I told you so" comes from people who never did. They want you to be right where they are…miserable and scared. Misery loves company.

Taking the leap can also give you a feeling of freedom. What usually prevents anyone from taking a leap is fear or doubt. When both are present, it really is similar to being in bondage. That "bondage" feeling can hold you back and keep you down. Taking the leap says, *"I trust in myself and believe in the possibility."*

Taking the leap of faith is perhaps the most powerful of the challenges. Sometimes with faith, you just call on a higher power other than yourself. I call on God. Whatever you believe, calling on your higher power when you lack belief in yourself can help you have the courage to follow through. Once you do, and you will be successful, it will be one of the most powerful feelings you'll ever have.

List some areas where you feel you need to take a leap of faith with courage to overcome.

1)_____

2)_____

3)_____

Philippians 4:13
I can do all things through him who strengthens me.

OBSTACLE #9 – ALMOST THERE AND QUITTING

I believe being almost to your goal and quitting is one of the most heart-breaking places for a person to be. Have you ever known anyone to be right there for their dream

and then quit? It happens to many people. In this story, you can see the young man was at the bottom of the mountain. Looking up, it looked too big for him, so he quit. This happens in life. People invest so much of their time, effort, and resources into whatever it is they wanted, then something happens and they give up. Just quit and let it go. Just when they were right there to get it done.

Has it ever happened to you? I hate to make you do this, but maybe writing down something you know you quit on, now you may be able to go back and complete it. Take a minute and write down at least one area you quit and see if perhaps, now is the time to finish what you started.

1)_____

2)_____

All of us have gifts and talents inside of which make us unique. Often, we start to work on an area we have a strong belief in, then end it. I believe, if you are still reading this book, you have built up new courage for what you want to accomplish in your life. It could be anything from mending a relationship, going back to school, completing that project, or anything you know you started and were right there to finish but didn't.

How do you get past, *"almost there?"* Never get to, *"almost there!"* You simply continue until you have what it is you've gone after. *Never stop! Never quit! Never give up! Never surrender!*

Develop the mindset that you will see it through. If it's important to you in the beginning, make it a priority to complete to the end. No matter what!

There might be some who will say, *"Well, at some point you may have to quit!"* I say, don't allow anyone else to determine when that time is. If you truly know and believe in your heart that you gave it all you had and you know you were so close, then be able to live with the result and not complain about it. Know you gave it your all. And who knows, you may be able to continue it at a later date if you want. *Just because you weren't successful one time, doesn't mean you can't revisit it later.*

2 Chronicles 15:7 – But as for you, be strong and do not give up, for your work will be rewarded

HANGING IN THERE

*T*he last two didn't give up. In the story, one of the kids slipped and was about to fall but the old man's hand reached out and grabbed her. It's an amazing illustration to see. When we think it is all over, or that we are about to fall, there is often cushion for us or something happens that prevents us from hitting rock bottom. Is it a coincidence?

No one really makes it on their own in life. Let's use professional athletes as an example. There are really talented professional athletes. Many have shared stories of struggles along the way and how hard they needed to work to get to where they are. In their stories of success, they reveal how they never gave up in order to get to their goal and destination. Although it's true for many of them, none of them would not have made it without help along their journey.

Help from others can include but is not limited to teachers, coaches, neighbors, family, and friends. Someone gave them an encouraging word. Someone else gave them clothing, food, and the emotional security to keep at their goal. Then of course, someone somewhere in high school, college, or the professional level gave them the chance to compete. Someone, somewhere, noticed them, and decided to give them an opportunity. A hand up.

That athlete just had to keep going for what they ultimately wanted.

In life, it's easy to think we made it on our own. We never make it on our own. There are forces of good which are always present to help. Just pay attention and begin to take notice. If you have successes in your life, did you really do it *all on your own*?

If you really think about it, can you recall circumstances in your journey where you thought something was coincidental? It wasn't. As long as you are pursuing the desires of your heart in a good way, there will always be an alignment in your behalf.

When we stay on our journey for whatever it is we're wanting to accomplish, there will be many obstacles along the way and there will be someone, somewhere, who will lend us that hand when we most need it. It may seem like a coincidence, but it isn't.

The person who offered you the job. *No coincidence.* The call you received for the extra money you needed. *No coincidence.* The credit on your electric bill you didn't expect. *No coincidence.* The person at the counter who paid for your coffee. *No coincidence.* The mechanic who didn't charge you fully for the service. *No coincidence.* The friend who called at just the time you needed. *No coincidence.* Whatever happened which showed you favor was no coincidence. It was, and is, part of the aligning for your path if you have the courage to stay on it.

What many of us go through won't be the same as what a professional athlete experiences. What makes your journey similar is recognizing as you continue, others will come along just when you least expect it to give you a hand.

How will you know this? Don't give up and you will see.

What you can know for sure is, by staying the course physically, mentally, emotionally, and spiritually, there will be success at the end. Your success won't look like any other's success. It will be special and tailored just for you.

WHAT IS YOUR GOLD?

*T*he amazing part of achieving your own personal gold is it can be anything you want it to be. I've mentioned along the way that your *"gold"* may not be anything

monetary. There are some of you who do want to gain financially and that's great! But for others, "gold" has a different meaning.

I once read a story of a very wealthy man who had all the money he could ever want. As a matter of fact, this particular man was a billionaire. He could buy anything he wanted and money was never a concern of his. However, he was missing something of more value than his money – Good, positive, strong family relationships.

This wealthy man had children who were addicted to drugs and one who committed suicide. His personal relationships were very poor. Only close people to the family would know why. Perhaps he spent so much time building his wealth that he didn't spend quality time with his children when they were small, or when they needed him. Maybe he didn't want children. Whatever the real reason was, it was publicly known his family ties were poor.

I believe, if he could have time back, he would probably want a better relationship with his family. After all, one can have all the money in the world but, if you can't enjoy it with people you care for, what good is it?

If he were on his death bed, and someone asked him what he wanted more of in all the world at that time, his answer would probably not be his yacht, million dollar car, mansions, or his money. Instead, in his final moments, he may want a closer relationship with those he cared for. What would you want?

From the list below, perhaps you can identify *"gold"* missing from your life. If there is nothing on this list, think about what you would like to achieve and add it.

1) Improved relationships with a family member
2) Continued education.
3) New job or career
4) New business
5) Improved health
6) Run a marathon, or compete in any athletic event.
7) Desire to move to a new city or state
8) Purchase a new home
9) Purchase a new car
10) Get custody of children
11) Travel to a particular destination
12) Overcome an addiction
13) Build a savings
14) Emotional wellness and balance

15) Spiritual growth
16) Lose specific amount of weight
17) Better marriage
18) Help improve your community
19) _____
20) _____
21) _____
22) _____

The key is to identify where you would really like to see improvements that are important to you and your personal growth.

Once you identify your gold, know the challenges and obstacles for any of them will exist. Be prepared to overcome them all and get your gold.

ONCE YOU HAVE YOUR GOLD

O nce you achieve your gold, the question may come up, now what? Once the better relationship is achieved, education completed, new career started, or whatever you identified as your gold, it will be key to first, maintain what you have. Secondly, identify another goal for your life and pursue more gold.

There is a song by a famous singer, and a line from it says, *"Big wheel keep on turnin."* I interpret the statement to mean that, as long as we have life in us, we should continue to strive to improve ourselves and help others. This is what I believe real life is about.

I believe people should always be reaching for some "gold" to achieve. For instance, once you start that new career and its going well, start to work on improving your health by losing weight and changing how you eat. Or, it could be a great time to get back in touch with that family member and create a better relationship. Perhaps you've retired from working 30 years with a company and instead of collecting your retirement check and watching television, take a few classes and get the degree or certification, and start your own small business on the side.

Whatever you can do to keep achieving, do it! Who said we have to live our life in one way? Who said once you retire you have to sit around and do nothing? Who said you can't go back to school at any age and learn a new skill? Who said once a relationship is bad it has to stay that way? Who said, once you overcome the addiction, you can't achieve something more? As long as you have life in you, you get to decide to improve every part of it if you want to.

It's your life! It's your time! You don't get a second chance so why not make the most of what you do have and become what you truly want.

Have better relationships! Have better health! Take the trip! Take the class! Save the money! Have the party! Do what you've held on to all these years! You have it in you. It's waiting on you to be bold enough and take the steps for your new journey. Go get your gold! It's going to make you feel good!

MORE NUGGETS

GETTING TO THE REST OF WHAT MATTERS

You're almost done! Congratulations! In anything you do or want to do, remember to always take a moment to celebrate along the way. It will encourage your journey. *Celebrate along the way is what I always say!*

My hope is you've read some information which has inspired you to take positive steps and action somewhere in your life.

I'm truly happy for you. Now, what you've learned, share it with someone you care for. That's what it's all about. Always be willing to share with someone you feel will benefit just like you did.

I've got some more nuggets to share. These nuggets are those areas in your life you can begin to look at to truly become the whole person you would like to be. It's about paying attention to the person you are and then discovering ways to become the person you'd much rather be. More Nuggets consists of additional comments I believe will add to your personal growth.

After serving in the Air Force, a few years later, I decided to take a new path for my life and get away from the freezing weather of Cleveland Ohio. While traveling to California, I knew I wanted to write. However, I became distracted. I thought I needed a job to make it instead of going on the gift which was given to me.

I've always felt I was supposed to contribute more but allowed everything in this book I talked about, every obstacle, to cause me to NOT pursue my dreams. I did write a poetry book, produced a music CD that combined jazz and poetry, wrote another book about relationships, and in 2016, I wrote a children's book called, "I Can," It's written in English and Spanish. You see, I'm still pursuing my gold.

Understand life is a continuing process and it's meant to be lived to the fullest. Circumstances will always challenge that process. We only really need to recognize there will always be moments which cause us to pause and wonder if we're making the right choice at the right time. It's okay to pause and ponder but not to stay stuck. This is what *"There's Gold on Top of That Mountain"* is all about: to give you the strength and confidence to keep it moving no matter what is going on with your life.

Get Re-fired Up!

I know "re-fired" up is not a real word. It can be if you want. It became real to me while listening to a radio show one day. A man who had retired, was talking about how he continued to work and build a business after retirement. It really fired me up about some areas of life.

Getting *"re-fired"* up simply means that wherever you are, you are deciding your life has more value left and you are deciding to dive in and give it another shot. It doesn't matter how old you are. I don't care if you're at the retirement age. I don't care if you are 90! It doesn't matter how young you are either.

If you want to be re-fired up, think about an area in your life you still want to have success. Don't allow your circumstances and where you are to define the rest of your life. You say, *"I know I'm here, but I have much more to do"* and you allow the fire under your feet to blast you into your goal!

Here's a nugget about age: My mother has always said that, *"Baby, age ain't nuthin' but a number!"* I've read where some people who are at the retirement age or older, only live a few years after retiring. Why is that? Well, it's been stated that some feel they've done all the work they want to do and believe they are done working. It's as if they believe their contribution days are over. What a bunch of crap! Feel that way if you want to. I say, *rediscover yourself after you retire and work on improving any area of your life.* Sitting around watching television, and talking about all your aches and pains is for the birds! Get a goal and work on it! Get RE-FIRED up!

The same goes for younger people. Get re-fired up! You have it in you. Stop sitting on your dreams. It's your time!

Younger people have a great advantage. You're young! You can make more mistakes and recover. You have the energy! Your brains are fresher. This technology at your disposal is exactly what you need.

Take advantage of your youth while you have it. If you haven't thought about the advantages you have, think on them now, and get out there and get re-fired up!

YOU ARE SHAMELESSLY FLAWED

I always hear people say, *"Well, I'm not perfect"* when speaking of themselves and justifying an action or lack of action. Of course no one is perfect! That's like saying, "I only have one head!" Claiming imperfection is obvious and it's negative. Claiming imperfection will also prevent a person from taking action in any situation.

Instead of claiming imperfection, try saying, *"I'm shamelessly flawed, but perfectly made!"* Acknowledging you have flaws is what being human is all about. When I say acknowledge your flaws, I'm referring to those physical and mental traits you have no control over.

You have no control over how tall you are, your color, any physical abnormalities, gender born with, or any other trait you may have which distinguishes you from any other person. So admit it! Own it! Flaunt it! Be you and as they say, *"Keep it pushing!"*

Being flawed doesn't mean you can't accomplish your dreams or goals. Being flawed actually allows you to be in a position to take the action you desire. A person doesn't have to wait on the "perfect" timing or circumstances. They simply act where they are.

Even the most successful super models, actors, professional athletes, or high level politicians are flawed. They just didn't allow their flaws to prevent them from pursuing their passions.

Guess what? You don't have to either. You don't have to wait on the perfect situation. Your time is now! Admit it and simply move towards your plan for what you want in your life. If you wait on the perfect timing, it will never come.

So read the following statement again, and allow it to sink into your brain:

I'm shamelessly flawed and perfectly made!

I'm shamelessly flawed and perfectly made!

I'm shamelessly flawed and perfectly made!

Never say, "I'm not perfect again!"

YOUR PAST DOES NOT DEFINE YOU

*T*he past can be the most destructive force for our present and future. I hear people talk about their past all the time. However, when we talk about our past, especially the negative parts of our past, we make it the present and bring those feelings along with it that stall our future progress.

A perfect example of bringing the past into the present is dating. I have friends and family members who regularly call me and share with me tales of their dating experiences. In just about every scenario they have shared with me how men and women bring up their past *failed relationships* as a measurement of how the new one should be. I would share with them, *"the people from the past are not the same people in the present!"*

I only used dating as one example of how our past can impact decisions we make for ourselves today. If those decisions are not allowing you to move beyond your present circumstances, you are stuck and will not thrive until you can move beyond them in a positive way.

It's easy to feel the hurt of the past, and then allow those feelings to impact your present emotions, thoughts, and actions. Professionals would describe it as a form of Post Traumatic Stress Disorder. PTSD is not only a military disorder. It's when an event from the past causes a person to experience stressful, and often negative emotions from that event which impairs them presently in one form or another.

I'm not discounting the seriousness of how our military are impacted from PTSD. I served honorably in the Air Force, so I am very empathetic to our military.

Recently, I sat in a meeting where the discussion was historical traumas, and how the past affects people today. While I totally agree that we shouldn't ignore the past as to not repeat it, I also believe focusing on the hurt and pain from the past, instead of the positive historic events during that time, in some way, permits people to justify and accept their current condition. As if to say, *"because this happened to me in the past, I can be this way currently."*

Our past, no matter what it was, no matter who you are, does not define who you are or who you can become! I say focus on the positives of your past and determine who you want to become. Determine the positive relationships you want to have. Determine what you truly want in your career, education, business, etc. Focus on the road ahead of you, not the road behind.

I once read, there is a reason the rear-view mirror in our cars is small and the glass in the front is so large. *Pay more attention to where you are and where you want to go, instead of where you've been.* I guarantee, you'll arrive to your destination faster!

TAKE NEGATIVE PRIDE OUT

Pride can be positive or negative. Positive pride is the feeling that comes along with achieving a goal you had or when someone you care about does something great. Like that feeling you may have watching your child graduate from high school or get recognized for being an awesome athlete. This is good.

The negative pride I'm referring to comes when one will not admit being wrong even when they know in their heart they were wrong in a situation. The prideful person says, *"I don't care how they feel, I'm right or even when I'm wrong, I'm not going to admit it!"*

When a person stands their ground because of their foolish pride, or believes they have the right to treat others bad, or continue to believe their self-righteous ways only matter, they really do more harm to themselves long term. It keeps you from maturing and growing into a true loving person.

Pride can an ugly monster. It has destroyed relationships. It has caused entire groups of people to know in their heart their actions were wrong with how they treated others but, would not admit it.

Getting past your pride requires one to humble themselves. To say, *"I'm not always right, and I can learn from my mistakes instead of repeating them."* Pride will keep you from experiencing the best you can potentially offer.

When you can recognize your errors and admit them graciously with a positive attitude, you will begin to experience the possibilities of your greatness. There is a powerful strength to humbleness!

Do you have areas in your life where your pride is preventing you from truly growing?

Write them here and work on being better.

1)_____

2)_____

3)_____

GET OFF THE FENCE AND MAKE A DECISION

Some people never get to where they thought they wanted to because they were never able to make a decision. Do you know anyone who always talks about what they are going to do "one day?" Are you one of those people? "One day" never comes around and an entire life can be lived saying, "One day!" Either you do it or you don't! Making a decision means to stick to it to the end. You want to have a better relationship with your children? *Start it*. You want to go to back to school? *Start*. You want to get another job? *Apply*. You want to save money? *Put some away*. Whatever it is you want to do, take action and stick to it. There is no other way.

What "One Day" goals do you have?

1)_____

2)_____

3)_____

Now, pick one and start working on making it happen. Make the decision to do it and make it come true!

Apologize and Free Yourself

O ne of the most powerful concepts to understand in life is the real power of forgiveness. Many do not believe this. I didn't always believe this. It took years for me to truly understand the power of forgiveness. Guess what? You don't have to delay your understanding another day. You are getting the real truth of forgiveness right here, today!

When you believe you've been wronged in life, there may seem to be a force which wants you to have anger, or hold a grudge to whom or whatever offended you. Naturally, many believe being wronged gives them permission to have hostile feelings, and hold on to them for as long as they want. This is probably the biggest lie to ever be told.

The resentment one holds onto does not impact the offender or the person to whom you hold the grudge against. True, they may feel bad about what happened, but the true pain felt will live in the person who could not or would not forgive.

To not forgive can cause resentment to build and spread within your body that's similar to a disease. When people don't forgive, it only makes them feel worse not better. Like a disease, not forgiving someone, can spread and cause more pain in your life. It can spread to people close to you and cause more anguish. The anger that comes along with not forgiving is unhealthy.

There are many benefits to forgiveness. There is the physical benefit of reducing the inner stress in your body that can cause other problems. However, the emotional and spiritual benefits of forgiveness can outweigh the physical advantages and have you in a better state of health and wellness.

When you forgive someone, no matter what happened, it frees your inner spirit to thrive. Forgiveness allows growth and prosperity within. It clears the air for new and flourishing relationships. Forgiveness says, *"I'm no longer going to be held captive to the pain and hurt. I choose to let it go, forget it ever happened, and love."*

Sometimes you have to forgive yourself. It may not always have been another who offended you. It could have been something you've done yourself and have kept the guilt of it your entire life. If you can't change it, forgive yourself and become a better person from it.

Forgiveness can be the new beginning for one person, a family, a community, or an entire nation! Forgiveness can be the shining star that lights the sky and gives clear direction for a new path and purpose. Forgiveness is power!

What do you need to forgive? Write it down here and go do it!

1)_____

2)_____

3)_____

Luke 6:37 – Do not judge, and you will not be judged. Do not condemn, and you will not be condemned. Forgive, and you will be forgiven.

GET OVER YOURSELF, AND HELP SOMEONE ELSE

Many people get caught up in their own drama and problems. *The "Woeisme" syndrome.* You have this going on at work, school, home, the child, dog, traffic, etc. Life is happening no matter what. Instead of focusing on what's not going good in your life, find someone else who may be in a worse place or in need, and do something for them.

I've found that when we reach out and do for others despite what's going on in our own life, we actually resolve our own dilemmas. Maybe not entirely, but taking the focus off of your own challenging situation and doing for someone else, has a way of reducing your own worries. Try it and see.

Can you think of a few acts of kindness you could do for others?

1)_____

2)_____

3)_____

REMOVE "LITTLE" FROM YOUR VOCABULARY

*A*long the personal journey, it's important to acknowledge every success you make without minimizing them. What do I mean? Each success you have is a giant step in getting to your gold. So celebrate it.

Try to form the habit of removing the word, *"Little"* from your vocabulary. I've heard many people describing an action they want to accomplish or something they did accomplish say, *"I did this little thing,"* or others will say, *"Oh, I see you have or did your little..."* Try to stop using that word when describing your success or someone else's success.

A person may not intentionally make the remark to minimize your success but that is exactly what is occurring. It's an intentional or unintentional attempt to disregard what you're ultimately wanting to accomplish. People who refer to anything you are trying to do as "little" may not have your best interest at heart.

Do not allow anyone to minimize the "gold" in your life. Trust me! They will try. Unfortunately, it will come from those who are closest to you. Be on the lookout for the *"minimizers"* and when the next person says to you, "Your little..." tell them immediately, *"These steps are huge for me and in the direction I choose to go!"*

WHAT YOU SAY TO YOURSELF IS TRUE

*I*n coaching clients or speaking at events, I practice listening to people all the time. When I have the opportunity, I share, *"words we say to ourselves and about our circumstance are real and true!"* If you want to really experience a true shift in the quality of your life, you must pay close attention to the words you say to yourself and others because they are powerful.

One of the words I hear from people many of the times are, "I'm so stressed!" It shouldn't be a surprise that stress is one of the top contributors of death. It's really not the stress that causes death, but stress is linked to other causes of death such as heart disease, cancer, suicide, and other ailments people have.

My purpose here is not to have a discussion about stress. This can be done at another time. However, I want to convey how important it is to pay attention to the words we say out of our mouths and in our heads.

Anytime we associate a negative word to our life, I believe we invite more of those circumstances into our life. For instance, if a person says, "I'm tired of being broke," what

I believe happens is the universe hears a cry out to receive more brokenness. All the universe heard was the word "broke," so it answers us by giving us more "brokenness." The universe wants to give us what we ask for.

The same applies when a person continues to say, "I'm so tired, worried, angry, or any negative word to describe how they are feeling. The universe only hears that word, and then it gives a person more stress, worry, fatigue, anger, and any circumstance complained about. Does that make sense?

If we change the words we speak, we can change the circumstances associated with those words. For example, instead of saying, "I'm tired of being broke," say, "I know abundance is in my future." What happens is the universe hears you requesting more abundance, and in return, creates situations around you that help you to receive more abundance. Maybe you find money on the sidewalk or in a pair of your pants pocket. Perhaps you get a call for a refund or a credit on your utility bill. The words you speak are powerful!

The same applies for every word you speak out of your mouth, or in your head.

Start asking for what you want, not what you don't want. It will take practice because a person gets so used to saying the negative words first. It becomes second nature. To turn it around and only ask for what you want will take pausing before you speak, being aware of what you say, and changing the thought. It will take practice.

One way to know if you are a person who says a lot of negative words is to carry a small notepad with you one day and each time you say anything negative, write it down. I challenged a person to do this once and they cried half through the day because they couldn't believe how much negativity came out of their mouth.

Try it for yourself and then change it. Once you do, you will witness your circumstances in every area of your life begin to improve. The new positive changes will happen and it will not be coincidental. They will exist because you changed the words you spoke to yourself. *Change the words, change the condition!*

What word or words are you currently saying to yourself that are not producing anything positive for your life?

1)_____

2)_____

3)_____

4)_____

5)_____

STRIVE TO BE CONTENT NOT HAPPY

I know I'll get plenty of people who will disagree with me here, but I believe it's better to strive for "contentment and/or peace" than "happiness."

Happiness is like that high one may feel during a peak period of an event. Let's take getting married for example. Not just getting married, but the wedding day. This is a day a person should feel really "happy," right?

Let's look a little closer. The wedding day can be chaotic. Really. Come on! Let's really look at it. The bride is getting dressed. People are running around to set things up. The groom is preparing as well. Family, friends, and planners are helping out. Other people are getting dressed and preparing to come as well. Everyone one is probably anxious during this *"happy"* moment.

The time comes where everyone is in their seat and awaiting the bride to walk down the aisle. Let's picture this beautiful moment. She and the groom are a little nervous. After all, this is the big day!

The Pastor says, "You may now kiss your bride!" Everyone *"Aws"* and is so happy for the newlyweds. This is happiness. But wait! How long did this "happiness" moment last? Exactly. A few minutes. All the other time was spent with nervous energy preparing for the event.

I'm not done. During the rest of the ceremony, food is eaten, drinks are had, people are drunk and dancing, toasts are given, and then later, after people are tired and sleepy, they all begin to leave. The "happiness" moment, with all the ups and downs, is almost over.

The honeymoon has "happy" moments, but the spending, preparing, and traveling are not necessarily happy times.

When the honeymoon is over and your back at home is when real life kicks in. The happy moment is over. Now, it's about adjusting to life, and everything it entails. This is where "content" reigns and kicks "happiness" to the curb.

Being content is experiencing life with the ups and downs and realizing that maintaining a level of peace is going to be where the majority of life exists. It's the place where we value what's around our lives, knowing it's not perfect, but recognizing it's manageable to the degree where we can live a fruitful life.

Maintaining *"happiness"* is not realistic. Some will use the term, *"sustainable."* We don't stay happy. We become content. Agree or disagree, I'd be willing to bet, if you truly evaluated your life, you'd discover there are more "content" areas than "happy" times. If you don't like the word, "content," replace it with "peace." It's okay to conclude being content is better.

You don't have to buy totally into it. There will be moments of "happiness" and those moments should be cherished! However, when you come down from that very high emotional place, understand you're coming to the "contentment" area of your life. Contentment will keep you at peace.

Philippians 4:11 -Not that I am speaking of being in need, for I have learned in whatever situation I am to be content.

GRIEF IS REAL BUT GIVE IT A TIME LIMIT

I won't try and pretend I know how long a person should grieve about anything or anyone. That is not my place nor is it my intention.

From my own experience, I can share my very recent grief for my Uncle Leon was a feeling I didn't have before. I've had relatives die. We all have. Many of those deaths happened when I was very young. I was close to all who had passed, but not as close as I was to my Uncle Leon.

When my Uncle Leon died, it hit me hard. Uncle Leon was more like a big brother. He was only four years older than myself and he lived with my mom and dad when his mother, my grandmother, died back in 1973. Uncle Leon encouraged me to join the Air Force, and he was an inspiration for me to write. He was also the one who introduced jazz and other music to me in the basement of our home on Stockbridge in Cleveland Ohio.

Over the last few years, we talked more often on the phone and by text. He and I hung out together when I was a teenager, and as an adult. I learned a lot from Uncle Leon, especially, in my younger years. We had conversations that can't be shared here but, they were always filled with laughter and cheer. It was good.

Before he died, I knew he was ill but, because I had spoken to him regularly, it was a shock for me when I received the call he had died. I had just spoken to him a week before and he was looking forward to my visit during the holidays.

My shock turned to grief, and then anger. I was not myself for an entire week and stayed in bed. Even after I returned to work, I still had this unfamiliar feeling. I couldn't function at work and could not talk to anyone outside of my mother and one of my aunties for a period of time.

This was honestly my first real experience with grief. I know earlier I spoke of my sadness when my dog died, but when a person you care for dies, there is no comparison to the grief one will feel. It also is different for everyone.

As hard as grief is, what I can share is grief is not meant to last a lifetime. It's meant to last for a short period. If a person does not limit their grieving period, it will be possible for the grief to turn to something deeper and more emotionally painful. I said it's possible, not probable. If you have goals you want to accomplish, you must allow yourself to begin to heal from your grief.

WHAT IS YOUR COMFORT ZONE?

I once heard a story about some cows who were corralled. There was a fenced-in area in a huge circle and filled with many cows. Each cow probably weighed at least a thousand pounds if not more. The fence was old and shabby, but it had been there for years.

One day an accident happened and the owners of these cows didn't come home. The herd of cows were running out of food. They just kept circling the area and eating on the ground where the grass had become nothing more than dirt. They circled and circled. Every now and then a cow would look up and view the green grass just on the other side of the fence. The cow would put his head back down and continue in circles with the other cows. This went on for weeks. One by one, the cows began to die from starvation. Again, every now and then one would look up and see the green grass on the other side but would not go over the fence.

Weighing over a thousand pounds would have been so easy for one cow to simply lean over the old fence and enjoy the plush green grass on the other side, but they didn't. Why is that?

The cows were so used to following each other. They did not dare to break out of their comfort zone. They were used to going in circles and following the other cows. One would think after seeing the green grass, at least one cow would have leaned over the fence. But oh no! They just kept in line with the other cows and eventually all starved to death. The comfort zone can kill you and your dreams.

Is your comfort zone keeping you corralled? Are you okay being where you are even though you realize every day that it's not what you want? The comfort zone is that place we stay even though we know it's not good for us.

What "comfort zone" areas do you feel are holding you back from living a better life?

1)_____

2)_____

3)_____

GET UNCOMFORTABLE IN YOUR COMFORT ZONE

*T*o change your comfort zone, you must get uncomfortable in it. It's easy to get comfortable in your life and the surroundings, even though you know it's not the best place for you to be. People do it all the time! Why? Because some feel the thought of changing a bad situation may result in a worse situation, so they believe it's better to stay where they are, rather than take the chance and do something different. Or they conclude, *"this is not so bad."*

It's crazy to believe the *"it's not so bad"* place is where many people reside. Are you one?

Getting uncomfortable is recognizing you no longer want to be where you are. It's understanding you are actually hurting any possibilities of a better life. A better life could mean better relationships, having a better career, a better home, a personal achievement, or anything you want in your life.

<u>Getting uncomfortable</u> may require getting rid of some people in your life. That's uncomfortable but may be necessary.

<u>Getting uncomfortable</u> may require giving up that food that's kept you overweight for all these years, or turning off the television and becoming more active.

<u>Getting uncomfortable</u> may require you to make that phone call to the relative or friend you haven't spoken to for years.

<u>Getting uncomfortable</u> may require you to register for that class and actually go this time because you want your degree.

<u>Getting uncomfortable</u> may require applying for another job and actually begin to prepare to go on interviews.

<u>Getting uncomfortable</u> might mean having a conversation with those deadbeats around you and asking them to leave and really mean it this time.

Whatever it may take, you have to become uncomfortable to get it done. But guess what? You don't stay uncomfortable. It only lasts for a little while. After you've become uncomfortable, an amazing thing happens: You become relieved and a new feeling arrives that creates a new comfort.

YOU DO NOT HAVE ALL THE ANSWERS

*I*t's okay to not know everything. I've always said if I get to the point where I know everything, then it means I am no longer learning anything.

It's funny to talk to a person who *"knows everything."* I believe teenagers believe they truly know more than adults. Do you know any teenagers who feel this way? My 17 year old daughter and 27 year old son are certainly two people who've expressed to me that my thinking is old. I just look at them with that side head look, and inside my head say, "How can a person who has lived so few years possibly know everything about life?"

Of course teenagers don't have all the answers. What they do have is the years they've lived to know whatever it is they've acquired. Many of them may have more knowledge of the technology they use. After all, they spend their entire existence on the phone, right?

Guess what? We don't have all the answers either. I believe we stop our ability to grow and learn when we believe we have all the answers in life. I'm open to learning from anyone and any age. I can learn from a five year old, and have taken the time to really pay attention when the "little" people are talking.

It's fascinating to listen to the children who are really just trying to figure life out themselves. We can all learn a lot buy listening to children.

Wherever you are in life, in order to continue to grow in every area of your life, begin to be open to the belief that you don't know everything and are willing to listen to others. You just might learn something.

STOP PRETENDING
EVERYTHING IS GOOD

Ever asked someone how they are doing? Almost 100% of the time you'll get the answer back, "I'm good, everything is great, or Ok!" While, I don't advocate sharing your challenges and struggles with every passing stranger or friend who inquires about you, I will strongly suggest that if everything is not ok in your life, don't pretend that it is.

There is a saying that goes, *"Fake it until you make it."* I believe that term is overused. Faking it until you make it? What does it really mean? Does it mean pretending your life is great even when it's not? Faking is not real. That's like someone saying, "The joke was not funny, but I fake laughed." Really! Faking it will not get you any closer to whatever it is you want.

How about "faking" your relationship with the person you truly desire to be closer to. How will that work out? Fake having a job and leave the house everyday while your family thinks you're actually at work. Fake going to the gym to work out. Fake saving some money. Fake taking a shower! Ok, you know where I'm going with this.

Faking it, or pretending everything is good, will not resolve our challenges. I would like to say, *"Work it until you got it!"* Doesn't that sound more promising? Feel free to start using that term instead of the other one.

Recognize there is a huge difference between "faking it" and "being positive and hopeful." When a person is faking it, they may not attempt to really work on improving themselves or the quality of their life. A person who is hopeful and positive is aware of their situation and they know it's temporary because they are working on improving those challenged areas of their life. See the difference?

It's okay that your world is not perfect. Guess what? No one's world is perfect. I like to say we should all be, *"Shamelessly Flawed!"* We are all here to do our best and let our best define us. Being shamelessly flawed says, *"this is who I am. I acknowledge and I'm not ashamed. I'm working on creating a better self!"* I share more on this a little later.

When you stop pretending and become open and honest to yourself about where you are, you may discover the truth will help you take those steps to improve your circumstances.

Now work with those flaws and become who you really are meant to be. You won't regret it. As a matter of fact, you'll realize your life will become better than it's ever been.

THE NAKED TEST

I had to follow "Stop Pretending" with the "Naked Test." The Naked Test will show you the absolute truth about how you represent yourself to the outside world. However, when you're alone, by yourself, you're someone else. People don't just cover up to clothe themselves. They cover up to hide.

It's easy to cover up. Just wear clothing that isn't too tight, and oh yeah, wear dark colors. We all know dark colors make us look thinner. If we look thinner, we look better to the outside world. The truth is, it only appears that way, right? As long as it looks like you're smaller or in better shape, you can get away with it.

The Naked Test is more than how we represent ourselves to the outside world. It can also be used to shed light on how we truly feel about ourselves on the inside. Do you think we do the same "cover up" on the inside? We cover up how we feel about our delicate relationships, career choices, and other important areas which create who we are. We cover our feelings and emotions.

What other areas in your life are you "covering up" that you need to conduct the Naked Test with to be able to finally make the changes to improve the quality of your life? Let's finally use the naked test to see our true selves and build to become better.

Take the real naked test and then take daily steps to change what's in front of you. Change your mental view of yourself and begin to recognize you have the ability to be free and thrive!

YOU ARE NEVER ALONE

People feel alone at times. In those moments, we can feel like no one cares for us. When a person feels alone, they may stop progressing and often get stuck in the lonely feeling. Well, I'm here to tell you that loneliness doesn't have to be real in your life.

Depending on what you believe, you don't have to ever feel lonely. Personally, I've come to the understanding that God loves us. He loves us no matter what. However, if we want His love, we have to believe there is a God, and the God who is the creator of everything in the universe and all the world can actually love each one of us individually as He loves us all. I believe that.

I'll add that the adversary is real. He wants you to feel like you're alone in those moments and he will put those thoughts in your mind so you can believe you're lonely. He wants you feeling lonely so he can be with you. His purpose is to kill and destroy. He doesn't care how long it takes but he'd rather you feel lonely the whole time you're alive so you won't do anything positive with your life. If you don't do anything positive with your life, there is a good chance those close to you, who look up to you, won't do anything powerful and great in their life either.

When your actions are halted because you feel lonely, no one wins except the enemy. See, many people who say they don't believe in God, and who fall victim to loneliness, anger, resentment, and other negative feelings and emotions, have a feeling deep inside which wants to self-correct their actions. What is that feeling then? It's God trying to get your attention.

God knows our hearts and He created us to do His will. His will is for us to love. When we love, everything we do will always correct our actions eventually. As long as we keep God in our hearts, we will never have to feel lonely.

I'll say it again, as long as we believe in God and know He is always with us, we never have to feel lonely. The enemy wants us to feel lonely so he can keep us for himself. Either way, you're never lonely. It just depends on who you believe in, and listening to.

Is it better to listen to the one who says, "Feel lonely, feel depressed, feel the fear," or is it better to believe in God and hear him say, "I am always with you so you can feel loved."

Matthew 28:20 – And behold, I am with you always, to the end of age.

97

THE NAYSAYERS

When you get to the point where you've decided to pursue your gold, there may be others who will say it's not possible or it can't be done. Don't listen to them. They are the *"naysayers"* who were not able to accomplish the same or more in their life, and they don't want you to either.

Don't be surprised if the "naysayers" are people you're close to. It's usually those who are closest to us who can discourage us the most. Why? Because we value their opinion and believe they have our best interest in mind. We listen to them, and more than likely will value their input. We want to please them, but later, when their input hurts our progress, we feel worse because we trusted them.

When people attempt to put down or discourage your dream, I say be aware of what they are doing. They may not do it on purpose. Some people are simply unaware. However, since you are a person who recognizes a "naysayer," I suggest you stop them and share, *this is your dream, not theirs, so stop trying to destroy it!"*

I can guarantee they will get on the defensive. Don't worry about it. Stay focused on your path and do not allow their negative vibe to touch you.

Do the Stuff You Don't Feel Like Doing

*I*f you're a person who wants to improve your condition and are wondering why it's taking so long, maybe it's because you PROCRASTINATE! Yes! Putting it off until tomorrow. Raise your hand if this has been you!

What I share with those who will listen is, *"Do the stuff you don't feel like doing and you'll live the life you will love!"*

When the words come in your head or out of your mouth, *"I don't feel like…"* this is exactly the time to do it. Fooling yourself and saying, "I'll do in later, or tomorrow, or any other time than "right now" will not happen.

If you continue to not do those tasks that you don't feel like doing, they never go away. As a matter of fact, it gets worse.

Don't believe me? Take a room that's cluttered. You walk in and say, "I'll clean it later" but don't. Each day the room isn't getting cleaner, it's getting worse. Clothes are piling up, and dust is building up. But you keep saying, *"I don't feel like cleaning."*

Not convinced. How about doing your taxes, going to the gym, improving a relationship, looking for a job, looking for a better job, starting that business, or anything else you can think of that you "don't feel like doing."

Imagine if you *"had done the thing you didn't feel like doing."* Can you picture how your life would be? Trust me. Doing what you don't feel like doing will result in a much more satisfying life. You won't have the stress on you. You'll experience the feeling of *"I did it!"* Once you feel that feeling, you will want to feel it again and again.

The next time those words, *"I don't feel like"* come into your brain, get up and say to yourself, *"This is exactly what must be done"* and do it! You won't be disappointed.

DEVELOP EMPATHY

*E*mpathy is understanding another person's position or feelings. When we begin to live our life with the thought that it's not always about ourselves, we can begin to experience a more rewarding life because we become more unselfish.

Some confuse *"empathy"* from *"sympathy."* Let me show you what the difference is:

Imagine you are taking a walk and you come across someone asking for help who has fallen down a hole and can't get out. Sympathy is saying, *"Oh, I see you down there. I'm so sorry you are down there!"*

In the same scenario, empathy is saying, *"Oh, I see you down there."* Then, the person demonstrating empathy gets down in the hole with them and says, *"Let's get out of here together."*

Empathy is feeling what another feels and being there for a solution. Empathy is really about action.

Sympathy is simply feeling for a person, but not doing anything. Now, there is nothing wrong with sympathy. We need to have it. I'm only saying to develop empathy more than sympathy because empathy is really doing something to help another. The more we do to help others, by default, we will receive more as well.

I don't advise helping others in order to expect help from them in return. It doesn't work that way. It works when you perform an act of kindness because you genuinely care. That's it. When you do for others, others will do for you when you least expect it.

T-B-W-S-K

Trust-**B**elieve-**W**alk-**S**ee-**K**now. This is the secret of success in my opinion.

When you have something you want to accomplish, how do you know it's going to work or if it's possible? You don't! There is an order to follow for your desires to happen.

You first have to trust. Now, what or who you choose to trust is up to you. If you don't trust in yourself, trust in a higher power bigger than yourself. Earlier in this writing, I mentioned this is not a religious book. It is one meant to inspire anyone to pursue what is in their heart. For me, in order to be able to complete this book, I had to listen to my heart and the powers of God to continue and finish.

When I felt doubt about what I was doing, I was not operating in my own trust. To operate in trust is an unwavering, unmistakable, indisputable confidence and assurance in Him and what He has planned.

Trust will look different for others and that's fine. You just have to operate in trust first. Trust will allow you to believe.

You must believe in your path, and believe strongly in order for it to come together. When we trust and believe, there is power in the two which allows one to take the action and walk in their belief.

Walking is taking the steps for your plan, idea, dream, or goals. Walking is action towards your purpose. As you continue to walk, you will see what it is you were trusting and believing in.

Seeing is the result of your walk, your actions, your belief and trust. Seeing is your desire coming true and then you will know.

You only get to know it at the end. If a person wanted to know what the end was in the beginning, they would never start. You can never know in the beginning.

Think about the Trust Fall. The Trust Fall is when a person standing with their hands crossed and eyes closed, falls back into the arms of someone, or a team of people who catch him. With the Trust Fall, one simply trusts he will be caught, and he believes either one person or a team of people will catch him.

When he walks (the action of falling) he then will *see* that he was caught, and now he *knows*.

The order of this can never be changed for success. If one tries to *"know"* first, the lack of that knowledge will keep them from ever starting. If they want *to "see"* first, the lack of seeing in the beginning, will keep one from ever trying. A person won't *"walk"* first without trusting or believing. It must be in the original order.

Think about it. Can *you* *"know"* how a relationship will turn out in the beginning? No, you can't!

Can you *"know"* if your new business will be successful when you first come up with the idea?

Can you *"know"* if you'll get the job, loan, or dream home? My point is, the order must stay the same in order for your desires, dreams, and passions to happen.

You also can not *"believe"* first. If you don't trust first, believing can cause one to have doubt. Trust allows belief. Belief does not allow trust. Think about these two statements:

"I believe he's truthful."

"I trust he's truthful."

Which one is more assuring? To trust is more powerful and confident in a statement or action.

In addition to the order remaining the same, it must stay the same throughout the journey. One can begin to trust, but if it's taking too long for results, one may give up, or want to jump to the end to know.

There are many stories throughout history of an entire population wanting to jump out of order and see results without continuing to trust and believe. Once you give up trusting and believing, the delay in you reaching your destiny will be on you. People delay their own success by not trusting the entire time.

As the old saying goes, *"Keep your eye on the prize!"*

I believe if you keep your thoughts fixed on the order of how it should go, you will complete all that you trust and believe in.

Know Where You Are in Order to Grow

Remember when you were a child and you wanted to know how fast you were growing? I do. I remember being excited when my mother told me to stand by the door in my room, barefoot, and she took a pencil to measure my height against the door frame. She'd mark it right above my head and then put a date on it.

That was my measurement at that time. After several months or yearly, she'd have me stand there again, and sure enough, I could see if I had grown or not. I remember the excitement I had when the measurement had changed. Did you ever experience that?

How about if a person wants to gain muscle or lose weight. What is the first thing they do? They either weigh themselves if they want to lose weight, or they measure the girth of their muscles to know what size they are when they started and know how much they grew from exercising.

With both examples above, in order to know if one has grown in height, or lost weight, or gained muscle, you have to know where you start. Once you know where you are, you can know what progress was made.

I also had to be honest. I remember being measured against the door and wanting the line to be higher. I would try and stand on my toes to make the line higher. My mother would tell me not to because it was cheating and it wasn't a true measurement of where I was.

To know if you are growing personally in areas of your life, whether it's managing your emotions or observing your life, you must take a real measurement or assessment of where you are.

You have to stand in the mirror and be honest with yourself about where you are in your life. No standing on your toes to pretend you're taller. You have to be totally honest and state where you are in the areas of your life you want to change or improve.

If you want your relationships with others to change because you feel they are not good, you must ask yourself about your true role. Are you being stubborn about something? Did you wrong someone and not go to them for forgiveness because of your pride?

If you were passed over for a promotion at work, ask yourself if you truly did everything you were supposed to truly be considered. Did you truly complete all the tasks you were asked to do, or were you really late or incomplete with a few assignments?

Do you find yourself living pay check to pay check but complain you don't make enough money? Could it be you're spending much of your check on items you really don't need? Be honest. Or, maybe you could be making more if you took the time to apply for other positions but you're not.

If you haven't lost the weight you've been trying to lose and you say, "Diets don't work," were you really being honest or did it not work because you weren't consistent with how you ate, or did you not exercise as much as you really should have?

These are a few examples of truly measuring or assessing where you are in order to grow. When we don't take that true measurement, we can't gauge how or if we're growing at all! We lie to ourselves and pretend everything is okay and adjust our lives to the lie.

Measuring where you truly are will open up the possibilities for you. It will have you thinking and planning for a better life. After the measurement, you can plan the steps to take, and this is where your life will become more exciting! Just like when you saw you grew just a little while standing against that door.

PEOPLE ARE WAITING ON YOU

I don't want to alarm you or make you feel guilty in any way, but here is something you need to hear. If you have a goal or idea that's stayed with you for a long time, you must complete it. Why? Because there is a population of people waiting on what you have, to impact their life. They are not waiting on anyone else. *It has to be you.*

Your idea, passion, gift, or whatever is in you that you're not using or doing, is supposed to impact others and it's not. I strongly believe this. This is why I had to complete my children's books, this book, the ones I've not written, and any poem I may have written. Although it has come through me, it is not for me. The same goes for you.

Imagine you're a song writer who wrote this beautiful love song but never did anything with it. Don't you know there is a person in the world who is waiting to hear the song you wrote for their life! That song could be what they need to start treating their family better, uplift themselves, relax them, or do what is needed to motivate or inspire them in another part of their life. That song is not for you. It's for them.

What if you had a strong urge to establish a real relationship with a family member you've not had contact with, but because of a family dispute, you don't speak about it. This feeling of wanting to be part of their life just doesn't go away. Guess what? The feeling is coming through you but it's not just for you. It may be for your families to connect and have strong ties many years from now long after you're gone. However, it had to happen through you. It's through you but not for you.

In the same way, when we don't utilize our gifts, and talents, we deprive many people we don't know from ever experiencing what those talents and gifts could bring to their life. Sure, you can say, *"My talent or gift is for me."* No, it's not! It's through you. It's for others. Be okay with this thought. It may be just what you need to keep the urge and passion to complete whatever is given to you.

Begin to work on those ideas because there is someone somewhere who needs what you have. We all have a responsibility to pursue those thoughts that stay in our minds and hearts. *"The gift given to you is a present for the world."*

FINAL THOUGHT

On the day I was completing this book, I heard on the news that Kobe Bryant and his daughter, along with other people had died in a helicopter crash. It was devastating news to hear.

He was an amazing basketball player but more than that, from the variety of newscasters covering this story, and the many others who knew him, he was a man who continued to pursue his gold. He wanted to continue to achieve so much more after basketball. He produced an award-winning documentary, wrote children's stories, and who knows what else he could have accomplished. My point is, he was pursuing it.

He was also a man who didn't allow failures from his past to define him. Instead, he accepted responsibility for his actions, but became a better person from it. He continued to thrive in the mist of obstacles and challenges in his life

I thought it was ironic that on the day this man was killed that I was in the process of completing my book about pursuing life ambitions.

I'm just a man with a message to share. I was given this message to share years ago. I don't know who it's for. I just know I was supposed to write this book and I am humbled to my core and appreciate you for taking the time to read, *"There's Gold on Top of That Mountain!*

We are all special people. We all have ideas, dreams, gifts, goals, or something we want to do and accomplish in some area of our life. I also know, the only way to make it happen is to start and never give up until you have what you desire. I know there can be reasons which can stall our progress, take a different path, or cause us to settle in life.

I say, "NEVER settle!" I don't care how young or old you are. As long as you have a strong desire for something, stay on that journey because if you settle, you will always wonder what could have been? You won't share it, but when you're by yourself, or in your own space, you'll think about it and probably regret not doing what you said you would do.

This book can be what you really needed. Don't procrastinate. Don't put this book down and go back to where you were. Let this be what you needed to fulfill whatever is in your heart in whatever area you are believing. I believe in you. You just have to believe in yourself.

I'm making myself available to you if you want. Sometimes, we just need someone other than those around to share with. I promise no judgement. I can just be the ear you need. Send me an email and I will connect. If you want to talk, provide your number in the email and we can set up a time to have a conversation as well.

Take care. I look forward to hearing about your success in any area.

My email address is e320wellnessandsafety@gmail.com.

Now get out there and make it happen! Get yours because, *"There's Gold on Top of That Mountain!"*

Made in the USA
Columbia, SC
27 May 2021